A CORONATION
WEEKEND ROMANCE

A ROYAL ROMANCE
BOOK 1

LAURA MARIANI

The
PEOPLE
ALCHEMIST

ABOUT THE AUTHOR

Laura Mariani is best selling Author, Speaker and Entrepreneur.

Laura writes non-fiction positive psychology success books for women in business and contemporary romance focusing on city life rom-com and billionaire romance books with a dabble of suspense.

Well, after all that hard work climbing the career ladder, you need to have some fun!

She writes strong female characters with backbone, big hearts and a stubborn streak. Every story has a happy ever after or a happy for now, and will make you laugh, gasp and cry a little.

Unless you have no sense of humour ;-).

Laura is based in London, England and, when she is not writing, she loves travelling, painting and drawing, tennis, rugby, and of course fashion (the Pope is Catholic after all).

Sign up for her newsletter for a free ebook and stay up to date on all latest Laura book news and blog.

You can also follow her on

twitter.com / PeopleAlchemist
instagram.com / lauramariani_author
Linkedin.com / in / lauramariani-fcipd

twitter.com / PeopleAlchemist
instagram.com / lauramariani_author
linkedin.com / in / lauramariani-fcipd

CONTENTS

1

THE VEUVE

Maggie woke up in her plush bed in the Deluxe Suite at the Gilbey, a delightful bar, restaurant townhouse offering a five-star bed and breakfast in the heart of Windsor.

She was making a quick pit stop in England to catch up with her old friend Sam before heading toward the Kingdom of Monois to cover the coronation of the new King over the weekend.

All remaining royal families worldwide would be in attendance together with prominent heads of State, a spectacle to behold.

Stretching in the big bed, she couldn't believe how far she had come: her trip was sponsored and fully paid for by major brands for her highly successful and influential blog "The Veuve", feeding the American fascination with all things royals, the pomp and the ceremony.

. . .

Maggie was living the life of her dreams, travelling first class, attending premieres, fashion shows, and a VIP in all major clubs. Who would have thought this was the same podgy shy teenager who once made a living serving tables and cleaning rooms?

She first met Sam at the end of her gap year backpacking through Europe.

England was her last stop before going back home to New York. After seeing the usual touristy places, she finished her year-long trip in Windsor, hoping to satisfy her childhood dream of seeing Queen Elizabeth, a real queen.

She spent a few months there, trying to make enough money to return home. Memories of serving behind the bar at The Reisse were flooding in. Sam was another barmaid there, paying her way through college, working weekend and evening shifts. They clicked immediately and stayed in touch ever since.

The Reisse was a pub in the town of Eton, on the opposite bank of the river Thames from Windsor, connected by a footbridge.

Eton, the home of the notorious all-boys boarding college, possibly the most famous public school in the world, founded by King Henry I, "the chief nurse of England's statesmen", educating generations of British and foreign aristocracy.

. . .

It was at the back of the Reisse that she lost her virginity to a blondish blue-eyed Etonian boy on a drunken night. She could have sworn he was a virgin too.

Maggie and Sam were doing a shift there on a bustling night.

A group of Etonians were gulping down pints and shots; they were loud and bolshy, as they mostly were in her experience. One of them caught her eyes. And she caught his. He kept glancing over, then winking. Then kept coming over to the bar to order more rounds.

Maggie hoped he asked her for more than just drinks. And eventually, he did.

"Can I wait for you when you finish your shift?" he asked.

"You're drunk", she replied.

"Indeed I am. Nevertheless, my dear, I still want to be with you; you are utterly beautiful", slurring his very poshly pronounced words.

"I'll think about it".

. . .

He kept asking, showering her with compliments and buying her drinks.

"You have beautiful eyes", he kept pressing, "and a delightful accent. Where are you from?"

"New York", Maggie answered.

She knew she couldn't play hard to get for much longer but was enjoying the game, for the first time feeling desired. Maggie had always been a tomboy, partly because she grew up with two brothers but mainly because she had always been insecure and uncomfortable with her weight.

His friends teased him whenever he went back and forward to their table; she could see him blushing.

"So endearing," she thought, smiling and feeling flattered.

When Maggie finished her shift, he was right there, waiting. She was thrilled to see him there; it hadn't been just all talk. He pulled her toward him and kissed her. His lips pressed onto hers, his tongue working his way.

"You taste so good", he said, "come ..." he gestured, grabbing her hand while they were making their way to the back of the pub.

. . .

He pushed her against the wall, fondling her breasts. She moaned. He fondled more. She kept moaning. He unbuttoned her blouse and leaned forward to suck her nipples.

"Ahi"

"Sorry", he whispered. "Did I hurt you?"

"A little", Maggie replied.

By now, their jeans were down to their ankles. Although that wasn't exactly how she envisaged she'd lose her virginity, she wanted him. Alcohol was for sure helping lower her barriers, but she couldn't deny she wanted him. Badly.

He was rough and sweet, passionate and clumsy. And quick.

Quick and messy, but she didn't care because he had made her feel wanted, desired and beautiful at a time when she didn't recognise herself as such. She seemed to remember he was good-looking but couldn't quite recall his face.

As he pulled his trousers back up, Maggie noticed a small tattoo on his groin, a yellow rose with something else intertwined that she remembered well.

· · ·

"That's cute", she said, thinking it was sweet.

"What is that?" she then asked, pointing.

"It's a C", and he could see Maggie's perplexed look on her face. "It's my mother's initial with a yellow rose, her favourite flower".

"She died not long ago", he added.

"Ah". Now that was creepy.

It didn't matter because she was smitten and falling for him. When they finished recomposing themselves, they walked back to the front of the pub, and there they were, his friends.

"He scored, he scored!!! Hip, hip, hooray! Hip, hip, hooray!!!" they screamed in unison, laughing.

"You owe me twenty quid", he answered, pointing his finger while walking toward them.

"The bet was a tenna", they said.

. . .

"Ten for the shag, the other ten because she is fat", slurring his words.

Maggie stood there, couldn't believe what she had just heard, tears streaming down her cheeks.

"M, come, they are all pricks, Etonian bastards," said Sam, passing a tissue. She had arrived just in time to hear it all.

Knock knock.

The sound from the door jolted her back.

"Good morning Ms Meddle", said the waitress with a smile on her face. Breakfast was here.

The young girl was standing there, looking at her like transfixed, with a stunned smile.

"Do you want a selfie?" Maggie smiled; this happened to her often. People recognising her

"Oh yes, please", the girl responded enthusiastically.

. . .

And so she obliged, glad she had already bathed and put some clothes on. Then, once she was alone again in her room, she ate her breakfast by the window, smiling.

The humiliation and anger of that night years ago were what she needed to start her new life and dream dreams she had never dared before dreaming.

Gone were the insecurities now and any real or perceived flaws.

"Girl, you look good", she thought, looking at herself in the mirror, happy with what was reflecting at her.

Her skin was glowing and tanned after a two-week trip to Barbados, her long dark hair tousled, her slim figure enhanced by skinny jeans and a simple white shirt and heels.

"Fat my ass, you arrogant prick".

2

THE PRODIGAL SON

"Faster, we need to go faster ... " he could see a car chasing them.

"They are on our tail", the headlight flashing in his rear-view mirror, almost blinding him.

"Stop, stop ..... Noooooooooo".

BANG.

Hupert woke up in a pool of sweat. The nightmares were becoming more vivid, the car crash still haunting him, with more and more memories flashing back each time.

Knock, knock.

. . .

"Mate, are you ok?" his friend Thomas on the other side of the door.

"I'm fine, thanks. I'll be down in a minute", he added.

Hupert was making a quick stop in Eton to visit and pick up his old school friend. After college and military service, he had spent years gallivanting around the world incognito, from Africa to ashrams in India.

Now, it was time to go back home.

His brother was about to become King. Their father's health was failing rapidly and too considerably to carry out the heavy duty of a King and Head of State. Maximilian III of Monois was abdicating to his firstborn, Prince Albert, his brother.

After the death of his mother, his father had become increasingly distant and withdrawn; he stopped even talking about her, Queen Carolina, as to wipe her off his and their memory.

He could not believe how the King and his brother continued allowing press members to cover royal events. The bastards had killed his mother and put him in hospital for months, chasing them like dogs down the road.

. . .

And now, he was about to go back into the folds of the Firm. He couldn't entirely accept or adjust to the fact that Albert was about to be crowned King.

"Why him?". The years in almost solitude, contemplation and meditation had done nothing to diminish the jealousy and annoyance of it.

Albert had benefited from all the privileges of his rank and even found love and happiness with his school sweetheart, Princess Violet, and had two children.

The Kingdom's future was now assured.

Albert looks so much like their father with his dark hair and piercing eyes and so unlike him.

And now he was returning to support his brother and perform his duty as was expected of him as a Prince and forth in line to the throne. Dutifully. Uncomfortably.

But before that, Hupert had to have a last swing at freedom and debauchery with his old friends. At least for a night.

The old gang was getting back together for a night at the Reisse.

. . .

The old pub.

Gosh, he still remembered the last night there before he had to be rushed off Eton because of a security incident.

To be fair, his memory was a bit fuzzy with all the drinking they had been doing. The last year in Eton was a blur altogether; after the tragic death of his mother, he tried to bury his head and feelings in alcohol. Lots of alcohol.

He only just about remembered the lovely and sweet girl behind the bar. She didn't treat him differently than anyone else. He relished that. She had beautiful eyes and a north American accent.

And great tits.

Yep.

Great tits; he remembered those but couldn't quite recollect if they ...

"H, are you coming or what?" Thomas was calling.

"I am ready", he responded. "Let's go".

. . .

And so they went out to meet the others, closely followed by the protection officer, his faithful companion everywhere he went.

3

HAVE WE MET BEFORE?

The Reisse had gone through some renovation; nevertheless, it was still the same old-style country English pub with local beers, wines and good old grub.

It was packed, as always.

The old gang was in their usual corner and had already gone through a few rounds when Hupert and Thomas walked in.

"The prodigal son", they shouted, aware of his travelling and distance from his family.

"Your f***ing Highness", Winston said, waving his hand and with a slight bow of the head.

. . .

"You are such a d***", Hupert answered.

"Oh la la", Thomas almost sang, pointing at the door.

"What a stunner".

H turned and saw what he thought was the most beautiful woman he had ever seen, a vision in jeans and a white shirt. Moreover, he felt warm, fuzzy inside, as if he had known her from before.

"Don't look. Cute guys at three o'clock," Sam said to Maggie.

"One looks a bit Neanderthalish with his fuzzy blonde-reddish beard and long hair".

"Yes, Old Etonians, but cute". Wow, he doesn't look like he belongs, Maggie thought. He was totally not the type of guy she always went for; he looked more rough and ready but handsome nevertheless.

"I know you're going to say it is strange, but he looks familiar".

"It is strange", Sam confirmed, "he is not the type you would know".

. . .

"But the type I could know", she winked.

"Oh yes".

"Hello, ladies", Hupert and Thomas said, greeting them both at the bar.

"Hello back", they answered almost in unison.

"Can we tempt you with a drink?"

"No, thank you. It's just a quiet girl's night out," Maggie said, dying to rip his clothes off but wanting to be chased.

"Have we met before?" Hubert then asked.

'You need to try a better line", she answered.

"I'm serious; you kinda look familiar".

"Nope, I'm sorry".

. . .

They kept looking at each other all evening, and Hupert sent bottle of champagne after bottle of champagne to their table, *Veuve Clicquot*, after seeing them order the first one.

After a while, Maggie went to the bathroom to refresh and top up her lipstick, leaving Sam at their table. When she came out, he was there, waiting.

"Hi".

"Are you going to make me beg?"

"Why not? It seems to come naturally …" she replied.

"Only because I know what I want when I see it, and I won't stop until I get it, whatever it takes", he said.

"Careful what you wish for; you might get it". How *cliché*; she should have thought of something wittier to reply with.

He came so close that she could almost feel the heat from his cheeks.

"Please … I am begging you".

"Maybe. Later". And then she left without turning.

4
___

A KISS IN THE RISSE

Maggie and Sam were having a great time, reminiscing about the old days and catching up on their latest achievements and news.

Samantha was an accomplished barrister specialising in commercial disputes.

"So, are you going to go for it?" she finally asked, dying to know.

"He has something about him besides his rugged handsomeness. He looks almost regal yet vulnerable", Maggie answered, not really answering.

"Crikey! How many glasses of champagne have we had? Clearly too many. I don't know about the vulnerable royal crap, but I'll give it to you, and he is handsome".

. . .

"Sooooo … Are you going for it?" She asked again.

"Perhaps".

"Ok, guys, I'm going to love you and leave you", Hupert said to the old gang.

"Shall I expect you later, H?" Thomas asked.

"Hopefully not", he smiled.

"You have the key, don't forget we are getting picked up for the airport in the morning", Thomas added.

"I won't".

He left the table and walked toward Maggie, the protection officer watching from afar.

"He is coming over", Sam pointed out. "It is now or never".

"I'm sure now is later", he said, looking at her deep in her dark eyes and grabbing her hand.

. . .

He led her toward the back of the pub and the stairs leading to the rooms upstairs.

"Where are we going?"

"I got us a room".

"You are so presumptuous," she said, annoyed but relieved as she didn't fancy a grope in a field at her age.

"I am indeed. Shut up, you know you love it," and then he kissed her, his beard tickling her face. The kiss was long, deep, and passionate.

"You are mine", and then he pulled her on his shoulder with one full sweep and carried her up the stairs.

5

IT IS YOU!

Finally. The room. He turned the key as quickly as he could, wanting to rip her clothes off as soon and as quickly as possible.

They started kissing frantically, hungry and thirsty for each other. He was glad she wanted him as badly as he did her. They were both playing a cat-and-mouse game, chasing and pulling.

The shirts came off, then the jeans. They fell on the floor, clumsy, but it didn't matter. They started there. She climbed on top of him, and began to move her hips, first slowly. Then faster and faster.

"Holy s***", he moaned. Maggie could feel him underneath her, growing harder and harder.

• • •

Maggie felt so powerful and inhibited.
And, most importantly, in control.

She kissed and licked his chest and bit his nipples, moving down slowly; he squeezed her bum and caressed her intimately between the cheeks.

She grabbed his boxers with her teeth and pulled them down. He lifted his hips as he couldn't wait a minute longer. He wanted them off. Now!

"Wow", she thought, seeing his penis now fully erect.

And it was then that she saw it; surely it couldn't be it. Surely not.

But it was—the same tattoo; a yellow rose with an intertwined C on his groin.

"Why did you stop?" no answer.

"What's wrong?" he lifted his head and saw a horrified and angry look on her face.

"What's wrong?" He repeated.

. . .

"You arrogant ... You, You", pointing her finger, now on her feet, "You Etonian prick".

"What have I done?", wait how does she know?

"You owe me twenty quid", she started imitating his voice and demeanour, "Ten for the shag, ten because she is fat".

And all of a sudden, it came back to him, twenty years ago, at the back of the pub.

Not surely, it can't be her. It must be.

She was screaming at him and gesturing while re-dressing herself at the speed of light.

And then she did the unthinkable: she picked up his clothes, threw them out of the window, and ran out of the room, leaving him there butt naked with nothing he could use as cover.

He got up as quickly as he could, still in shock, frantically looking for his phone when there was a knock at the door.

He opened it sheepishly.

. . .

"Your Royal Highness, is there a problem?" the protection officer was there; thank God for that.

"I need some clothes", he said without explaining.

"Yes, Sir, I'll be back shortly; wait for me here".

"As if I am going to go anywhere like this," he thought, shaking his head.

He needed to find her, but she had vanished, and there wasn't time.

The following day he was leaving Eton and flying back to Monois to attend the banquet before the coronation to welcome all foreign dignitaries.

Maggie ran across the footbridge back into her hotel, tears streaming down her face. All the feelings she had repressed for so long bubbled back up with all her insecurities.

Thankfully there was no time for regrets or mulling over; she had to prepare for the biggest live stream of her life: the coronation of King Albert II.

6

THE SECRET PRINCE

The Coronation Order of Service at St Anne Cathedral.

Their Majesties, The King and The Queen Consort, will arrive at the Cathedral in procession from the Palace, known as 'The King's Procession'.

After the Service, Their Majesties will return to the Palace in a larger ceremonial procession, known as 'The Coronation Procession'.

Other Members of the Royal Family will join their Majesties in this procession.

At the Palace, The King and The Queen Consort, accompanied by Members of the Royal Family, will appear on the balcony to conclude the day's ceremonial events.

Hupert was looking at the official palace's announcement, dreading to meet his family; it had been years since he had seen his father, brother and his beloved grannie, Queen Cecilia.

Fortunately, there was little time for deep discussions between the banquet and the fact that he had to attend rehearsals for the procession and the coronation.

He knew, however, that the time would come sooner or later. But that time was not now.

First, though, the last-minute fitting and check for his ceremonial uniform. He had missed not being in the military, perhaps the only thing he did miss during his travels.

"The beard needs to go", Queen Cecilia declared, saying what the others didn't dare express,

"and a good haircut, too. You need to look like you belong in that uniform".

"Yes, grandmother", he replied, understanding there was no point in arguing.

His father looked frail and tired, leaning on a walking stick whenever he could and when others were not around. His skin was grey and thin, almost translucent.

. . .

His brother, on the other hand, was as handsome as ever. His wife, Princess Violet, soon to be Queen Consort, was making last-minute preparations and chose to incorporate elements into her dress to honour their late mother.

It was thoughtful but also annoying. It was his mother.

Everybody seemed to have continued their lives as if nothing happened, but he couldn't let go and forgive or forget.

Hupert recalls the precise moment he woke up in his hospital bed and was told she had died at the scene. The days that followed were filled with physical pain from physiotherapy and a sense of void and emptiness.

The state funeral was a spectacle; the whole kingdom and half the world had shown up to say goodbye to his beautiful mother, the Hollywood starlet who married the dashing playboy Prince of Monois and then became a Queen, not just on the silver screen, but in real life. Americans especially were obsessed with her.

After some suitable time, he had returned to Eton and thrown himself into parties, drinking and some pills occasionally—anything to numb the pain and not feel.

. . .

He tried to remember what had happened, but everything was a blur for a long time—everything but the black car following them at speed.

And now, he was back for another state event: the new monarch's coronation, the formal investiture with regalia and crowning in the main Cathedral.

His brother was about to become King. So, from tomorrow, Hupert must bow before the King and his wife.

"Dammit".

"H, you good?" Thomas asked. Thomas, the Duke of Monisque, his long-life Etonian friend who had listened to all his gripes and fears for the last twenty years or so.

"I'm good. Let's do this".

On the eve of the Coronation of King Albert II and Queen Violet, the Monois Royal Family was hosting a Reception at the Palace for Foreign Royalty and Heads of State who were in Monois to attend the Coronation. It was also the evening when Hupert was making his official comeback, standing side by side with his family.

"Your Majesty", Hupert greeted King George III of Saint Moncito, a long-distance cousin of his father. The two seemed to try to avoid each other as best they could. Their feud was common knowledge, although nobody knew how or why it started. Nevertheless, duty is duty.

"Nice to see you, Your Highness; glad you are back", he responded.

Hupert nodded.

"You seem distracted", Queen Cecilia whispered.

"A lot to take in", he answered.

"Seems to me more like girl trouble," she said with a wink in her eyes.

Hupert couldn't believe his ears. He had been thinking about her all day and night.

"I have seen that look before. In your father when he met your mother. Something I should know?" she added.

He was about to answer when a flash went off in his face.

"Your Highness, they are doing their job," his protection officer quickly intervened, realising he was about to kick off.

• • •

"They have been invited to cover the events".

He had to leave the room and splash cold water on his face —the sounds of sirens in his ears.

"H ... H?" Thomas had followed him into the bathroom with his guard.

"I am good, I am good. For a second, I thought I heard ambulance sirens."

"I just need a minute", he then added.

Commander Philips nodded and made a quick exit. He had to see the King.

"Your Royal Highness",

"Commander".

"The time is near, Sir".

"Thank you, Commander", King Maximilian answered. Hupert was beginning to remember. It won't be long now, and it couldn't have happened at a worse time. He had been dreading this moment for the last twenty years.

. . .

Maggie had also arrived in Monois to cover the coronation, wanting to focus firmly on her job and trying to soak in the momentous occasion.

The Coronation of His Majesty The King and Her Majesty The Queen Consort will occur at St Anne Cathedral.

As previously announced, the Service will reflect the Monarch's role today and look towards the future while rooted in longstanding traditions and pageantry.

Usually, a coronation would be a symbolic formality and not signify the official beginning of a monarch's reign; *de jure* and *de facto,* the reign would commence from the moment of the preceding monarch's death, maintaining the legal continuity of the monarchy.

But in this case, King Maximilian III was abdicating.

Additionally, all other European monarchies have abandoned coronations favouring inauguration or enthronement ceremonies, making this event even more extraordinary.

Maggie knew she was lucky to be here. She would have loved to be at the reception tonight but wasn't 'official press' and, therefore, not invited to cover.

. . .

She had, however, secured the best place in town tomorrow to watch the procession go by and carry out her live stream.

She was so excited she could barely sleep. Oh yes, and him. The asshole who took her virginity for a bet, and she almost fell for, once again, last night.

"Margaret Meddle: what's wrong with you?" she said sternly to herself.

"Tomorrow is a big day, don't mess up. And who knows? You might even meet your prince charming with all the royals and aristocrats in town.",

"Universe, I'm open for some magic in my life", she declare before finally going to bed.

Maggie woke up bright and early; her make-up artist and stylist were in her room helping her getting ready. She couldn't disappoint the brands sponsoring her trip and coverage of the coronation and was making sure she was the perfect brand ambassador.

She had the perfect spot, near the CNN and BBC crews.

. . .

The day he had dreaded was here. Finally, his brother would be King, the job he had prepared for all his life. And now that he had two children, his place in the succession line had gone even further. Hupert was really and truly a spare now.

"Let's get this show on the road", he thought.

The Queen Mother, his Father, brother, and his wife were all taking position so the procession could begin.

Hupert took his place and boarded the armoured royal car.

"Here we go".

The streets were lined up with people four-five deep; they had camped for days waiting.

The Royal family would be the last to arrive in the Cathedral after foreign royals, politicians, and, finally, the soon-to-be King and Queen.

"Your Royal Highness?" said his protection officer sitting in the front seat.

"Yes, Commander?", Hupert answered.

. . .

"You are meant to smile and wave, Sir".

"Oh yes, I forgot."

"It is a glorious day out here, " Maggie told the camera. "The sun is shining, it is warm, and the atmosphere is priceless.

"The procession is about to pass by. But, wait, wait ... I can see a royal car arriving."

People started screaming.

A handsome blonde royal was waving to the crowd.

"Prince Hupert, Prince Hupert", young girls were screaming.

He turned his face, and then she saw him. Without the beard and the long hair, but definitely him. In a royal car in full ceremonial regalia.

As he waves around, he saw her too.

"He is a Prince".

7

THE TWAIN

T he car had arrived in front of the Cathedral.

"Sir"

"Sir, you need to get out of the car".

Hupert was transfixed. She was there, covering the coronation. Perhaps a member of the press, his more dreaded profession.

"Oh yes," Hupert replied.

The door opened, and he stepped out. Cheers and screams left and right. A glance, a smile and a wave.

· · ·

And he was in. Hupert took his assigned place and waited for the rest of the procession to arrive. He had to talk to Thomas.

Everything seemed to go so slowly.

A set ritual steeped in history: the Recognition, the Oaths, the Anointing, the Investiture and Crowning, and finally, the Enthroning and Homage.

He had to concentrate and perform his duties, including swearing his allegiance to his brother, the King.

Maggie was trying to remain calm and act like nothing happened whilst interviewing members of the public who were keen royalists.

The prodigal son had returned, Prince Hupert of Monois, soon third in line to the throne.

She had lost her virginity to a Prince—still an asshole, but a royal asshole.

Hupert couldn't wait for the day to be over. There was still the long procession to come and the salute from the balcony, followed by a lunch.

. . .

He had to find a way to reach her. He believed in destiny, and the fact that he met her on his first day back in the same place, the same town, spoke volumes to him. She was special. It was meant to be.

The cameras were following the royal family's every move and expression. Hupert couldn't think of more painful torture.

Smile, wave, and appear interested. More smiling.

The service was over, and as they made their way out of the cathedral, he turned and looked straight into her eyes.

"Sorry", he whispered with an almost imperceptible move of the lips before taking his place in the hundred-year-old royal carriage.

She stared back.

The second ceremonial procession was grander, longer, and more pompous. Hupert had been away so long that he had forgotten the restraint and patience one has to exercise to go through these events.

Hupert couldn't remember her name.

· · ·

"Oh God, did I ever ask her?"

The horrified look on her face when she recognised his tattoo told him he had not exactly been a gentleman. His Eton days had not been his best. It's a miracle he managed to finish school and not get arrested in the process.

Hupert didn't want to lose her. She still had the most beautiful tits. Those he remembered well.

Maggie had to continue with her live stream until the end of the day. Guest after guest, interview after interview. Everything was a blur.

"He said sorry", she was thinking. "Did I imagine it?"

"Sorry for what? For having sex with me for a bet? For not telling me he is a Prince?" well, she could understand that one.

"For not at least apologising the days after? Sorry for what?"

The official order of the day was finally coming to an end. Now he had to find her.

. . .

"Commander, I need a favour", he said, approaching his protection officer after the salute from the balcony.

"Yes, Sir".

"Outside the Cathedral, on the right-hand side, there was …", and before Hupert finished talking, he handed him a piece of paper.

"What is it?" looking perplexed.

"The hotel where Ms Margaret Meddle is staying with her room number".

"How did you … never mind. Thank you, Philips, thank you".
    The Commander nodded.

Maggie was back at her hotel; she had ordered room service, she couldn't bring herself to mingle with people.

Knock knock.

She opened the door, thinking it was her dinner. But it wasn't. It was instead a humongous bunch of flowers.
    And the some more flowers and more flowers after that: apology flowers and red roses.

. . .

Lots of red roses.

Her room was now covered with flowers. She had no time to sit down when there was another knock on the door.

"Yes", she said as she opened the door.

"A man desperate to be forgiven by the woman he loves has got all the flowers on sale", he said, standing there with a single red rose in his hand.

She knew then that some magic would enter her life and the twain be made one.

EPILOGUE

The next day, Hupert had invited Maggie to the Palace; the Royal Family was hosting a garden party, this time with no press, only royals and aristocrats from around the world.

H was keen to introduce Maggie to his family and friends and for her to see him in 'his environment'.

"Remember, you need to curtsy in front of my family and everyone at that party.

Just the first time you greet them".

"What? Do you ..?"

"Yes. Even royals bow and curtsy to the King and Queen—and anyone who outranks me. You'll see, all royals greet each other with a bow or a curtsy".

. . .

"I am an American", she said.

"You are not in America now but meeting the Royal Family", he replied. "That's the way it is, darling".

"You are going to be fine, don't worry, they'll love you", trying to reassure her.

His brother was polite but distant, his wife warmer and more welcoming.

"What a sight for sore eyes", Queen Cecilia proclaimed. "I knew it" Looking at him to say, "See, I knew".

"Grandmother, this Ms Margaret Meddle from New York", Hupert said, introducing her.

He quickly pulled her back as he could see she was going for a hug, trying to signal to curtsy.

"It's quite all right, my dear", she said, " Hupert, I don't bite".

They walked out into the palace garden side by side. "Follow my lead", he whispered.

. . .

So many people he had not seen since childhood were there, including Princess Victoria of Moldof, who used to tease him mercilessly, his once promised one.

"Your Royal Highness", she greeted him with a curtsy.

"Your Royal Highness", he replied with a bow.

"Ms Margaret Meddle", he introduced her.

Maggie curtsied.

"How delightful".

Mwah mwah, and she walked off.

"What was that?" she asked him.

"Don't worry. Victoria doesn't like many people".

"Who is that?" the princess asked Thomas, Duke of Monisque.

. . .

"Hupert's new girl", he replied.

"Mmmm", sipping champagne.

"Victoria ... don't be mean", he said.

"I don't know what you mean, Thomas darling".

Overall, the day went smoothly, and Maggie managed to survive it. After supper, they retired to his apartments in the palace.

"Wow" her mouth wide open. "Wow, wow, wow!!!"
    "This is yours?" she asked.

"It's a royal palace belonging to the Crown and the State. My family's. I use these", he answered.

"Let's go to bed. I've wanted to kiss you all day".

"Just kiss?" she smiled.

He took her in his arms and threw her on the bed.

· · ·

"Not quite, my dear. I'm going to f*** you all night like there is no tomorrow".

"Your Hardness, yes, please".

And so he did. The fell asleep wrapped in each other he was still inside her. Until …

"Nooooo ….. "

"H, wake up, wake up. It's a dream," Maggie said, touching his arm.

"I killed her. I killed her", he was shouting.

"It was a nightmare, baby; it is not real", she said, trying to soothe him.

"No, no. I killed my mother. I remember now. I was driving, I killed my mother".

NEXT IN SERIES

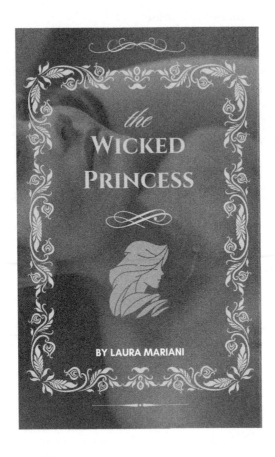

CONTEMPORARY ROMANCE BY
LAURA MARIANI

The Nine Lives of Gabrielle - a whirlwind romance and a journey
of self-discovery - the perfect city-life romance to make you laugh
(unless you have no sense of humour 😊), reflect, gasp, and
perhaps shed a little tear while enjoying the excitement of the Big
Apple, dreaming of Paris and longing for London.

ALSO BY LAURA MARIANI

I don't care if you don't like me: I LOVE ME - 28 ways to love yourself more", - a self-love book with guided practices for women inspired by my contemporary romance book, **The Nine Lives of Gabrielle,** and the journey of self-discovery and self-love of the protagonist, Gabrielle.

Here you will find 28 quick and easy ways to love yourself more every day with techniques that you can try out and then adopt going forward.

Day by day, all these little practices stack up and compound, creating a domino effect, not visible at the beginning but with a massive impact as you move along.

And then, just like that, everything in your life **WILL** change ...

NON-FICTION BY LAURA MARIANI

90 Days To Reboot Your Career: How To Reinvent Yourself, Your Career And Your Life

The **90 Days To Reboot Your Career** book contains techniques and exercises that demonstrate that you do not need to be defeated by anything and have precisely what you want.

It is laid out as a journey for 90 consecutive days with new exercises specific to the area tackled (Think, Look or Act) and a bonus.

The first 30 days will nudge you step-by-step along the way to upgrade your mindset and make winning an essential part of your life and business (Think).

The next 30 days will show you how to elevate your brand and present your unique Best Self, a key part of your life and business (Look).

And finally, the last 30 days will guide and assist you to act despite fear, with challenges to push your boundaries (Act).

A practical and clear, direct-action personal improvement guide to help every woman to achieve what she desires in her career.

The **90 Days To Reboot Your Career Planner** mixes Law of Attraction / Assumption with positive self-image psychology, enabling and supporting your empowerment, in true alchemist style.

The planner is laid out as a journey, from the big, longer-term 5 years vision and goals down to the yearly and monthly breakdown of your business vision and goals.

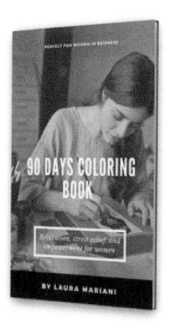

The **90 Days Colouring book** is the perfect accompaniment to the **90 Days To Reboot Your Career** book and planner and also a stand-alone vehicle for relaxation and stress relief.

In both cases, it is a tool to enable you to exercise some self-care when you need it most. Or just for fun.

Whatever you are currently juggling (career, family, health, relationships) it is important to always take time for yourself. Love yourself first. Take care of yourself first.

For new releases, giveaways and pre-release specials check www.thepeoplealchemist.com

You can also buy Laura's books directly from Laura Mariani at www.payhip.com/LauraMariani

DISCLAIMER

A Coronation Weekend Romance is a work of fiction.

With the exception of public places, any resemblance to persons living or dead is coincidental. Space and time have been rearranged to suit the convenience of the book, memory has its own story to tell.

The opinions expressed are those of the characters and should not be confused with the author's.

AUTHOR'S NOTE

Thank you so much for reading *A Coronation Weekend Romance.*

I hope you enjoyed the story. A review would be much appreciated as it helps other readers discover the story.

Thanks.

Places in the book

I have set the story in real places like Eton and Windsor and the fictional kingdom of *Moinos*.

You can see the places/mentions below - find out more about them or perhaps go and visit:

Gilbey's Bar, Restaurant and Townhouse
Eton
Eton college
Windsor Castle

Printed in Great Britain
by Amazon